Let's Pick Apples

By Jenne Simon
Illustrated by Prescott Hill

SCHOLASTIC INC.

ISBN 978-0-545-53182-5

12 11 10 9 8 7 6 5 4 3 2 1   13 14 15 16 17/0

Designed by Angela Jun
Printed in the U.S.A.   40

First printing, August 2013

The weather in Lalaloopsy Land was perfect. *It's a great day for spending time with friends,* thought Pepper Pots 'n' Pans.

Luckily, she'd already invited some friends over.

DING-DONG!

Berry Jars 'n' Jam, Sunny Side Up, and Blossom Flowerpot had arrived.

"Thanks for inviting us over," said Blossom.

The girls were excited to spend the day together.

But they could not quite agree on what to do. Each girl had her own idea for a fun activity.

Berry and Sunny wanted to play outside.
"We could go on a hike," suggested Berry.

"Or ride our bikes," added Sunny.

"I'd like to be outside, too, but I'd rather work in the garden," said Blossom.

And Pepper wanted to cook the girls a sweet treat to share.

"How will we ever all agree?" she asked.

"I know," said Berry. "Let's go apple picking a
the orchard!"

"That's perfect," said Sunny. "Now Berry and
can spend the day outdoors."

Blossom smiled. "I'll get to work with plants,"
she said.

"And I'll make us a delicious snack with the apples!" cheered Pepper.

"What will you make?" asked Sunny.

"And can I help cook?" Berry chimed in.

"Of course," said Pepper. "But the menu is a surprise."

Soon the four friends arrived at the apple orchard.

They saw lots of tall, leafy trees filled with red and yellow apples.

"I can taste the crisp sweetness of the apples already!" said Pepper.

"Me, too," said Berry. "But first we have to pick them!"

"Then you better climb up here," a voice called from above.

It was their friend Forest Evergreen!

"Would you like to help us pick some apples?" asked Blossom.

"Pepper and Berry are going to make us a treat with them," added Sunny.

"What kind of treat?" asked Forest.

"It's a surprise," Pepper said with a smile.

"I like surprises!" said Forest. "Of course I'll help."

He began to pick the apples nearest to him and gently tossed them down to Sunny's waiting basket.

Pepper watched her friends picking perfectly nice apples from the trees.

But her eyes were drawn to a cluster of huge shiny red apples at the top of the biggest tree in the orchard.

"I just have to have some of those apples for my kitchen!" she shouted to her friends.

"But how will we reach them?" asked Berry.

"I will get them for you," Forest told Pepper. Forest was the best climber in Lalaloopsy Land He scrambled up the tree, jumping from branch to branch.

Blossom tossed her lasso high into the air.

The loop caught on a giant red apple.

But the daisy chain was not strong enough to pull it free.

It fell apart in Blossom's hands.

"Maybe my butterfly can help knock down the apples," said Blossom.

Butterfly tried her hardest.
But she was not strong enough to knock the apples down.

"We need to work together," said Berry. "And
know how."

She got down on her hands and knees, and
smiled up at her friends.

"Let's make a pyramid," she said.

Everyone joined in . . . even the pets!

Forest climbed to the top and stretched up on his tippy-toes.

But he just as he was about to snag the apples, he lost his balance.

"We'll never reach them!" Pepper cried. "My sweet surprise is ruined!"

"Do you need some help?" a voice called. It was Ember Flicker Flame, the bravest firefighter in Lalaloopsy Land.

"We do," said Pepper. "I need apples at the very top of this tree to make a special treat." "But we can't reach them!" added Berry.

"I have something that can help," said Ember. She rushed off, and moments later returned with the tallest ladder from her firehouse.

Ember scurried up the ladder. Then she picked the shiny red apples from the top of the tree.

"You saved our snack," said Pepper. "Let's head to my house to start cooking."

Berry and Pepper were hard at work.

Pepper had finally told Berry what was on the menu: homemade apple pie and fresh applesauce.

Berry started by rolling out the pie crust, while Pepper stirred the pot of applesauce on the stove.

While Pepper and Berry cooked, the other friends set the table.

They could smell the sweet scent of apples wafting in from the kitchen.

Finally, the snacks were ready!
"This pie is delicious!" said Ember.
"So is the applesauce!" added Forest.

"I'm glad we picked the best apples," said Blossom.

Pepper smiled. "I'm glad I picked the best friends to share them with!"